For Linda,
a celebration

Scholastic Children's Books,
Commonwealth House, 1-19 New Oxford Street,
London WC1A 1NU, UK
a division of Scholastic Ltd

London ~ New York ~ Toronto ~ Sydney ~ Auckland
Mexico City ~ New Delhi ~ Hong Kong

First published by Scholastic Press,
an imprint of Scholastic Ltd, 1999

Text copyright © Brian Patten, 1999
Illuminated letters, title page, cover artwork © copyright Siân Bailey, 1999
A, B, C © copyright David Armitage, 1999
D, G, V © copyright Tim Clarey, 1999
E, N © copyright Patrick Benson, 1999
F, I © copyright David Parkins, 1999
H, M, R © copyright Cathie Felstead, 1999
J, T, Z © copyright Karin Littlewood, 1999
K, Q, W © copyright Helen Ward, 1999
L, O © copyright Jane Ray, 1999
P, S, X © copyright Jason Cockcroft, 1999
U, Y © copyright Nick Maland, 1999

ISBN 0 590 11389 5

Printed in China

All rights reserved

2 4 6 8 10 9 7 5 3 1

The author and artists have assserted their moral rights.

THE BLUE & GREEN ARK

AN ALPHABET FOR PLANET EARTH

by

BRIAN PATTEN

with illustrations by

DAVID ARMITAGE, SIÂN BAILEY, PATRICK BENSON, TIM CLAREY,
JASON COCKCROFT, CATHIE FELSTEAD, KARIN LITTLEWOOD, NICK MALAND,
DAVID PARKINS, JANE RAY *and* HELEN WARD

SCHOLASTIC
PRESS

A is for Ark,

For the blue and green Ark adrift in the dark.

B is for Beginning, for the birth of all that surrounds
The blue and green Ark adrift in the dark.

C is for Cauldron,

For the earth's cooling core and the creation of all

On the blue and green Ark adrift in the dark.

D is for the Dinosaur and the Dodo,
Symbols of all that have long vanished

From the blue and green Ark adrift in the dark.

E is for the Eagle and its eyrie,

And for the eggs the eyrie shelters.

It is for the emerald and elderberry,

The emu and elephant.

It is for the eye that can see all things

On the blue and green Ark adrift in the dark.

F is for the Fire around which Neanderthal man crouched,

For the flames that kept at bay the sabre-toothed tiger,

The perishing cold, the unknown demons.

It is for the flight of migrating birds and the frontiers beneath them,

For the fish, floating like golden submarines beneath lily-pads.

G is for the Gorilla snuggling down in its gigantic nest,

For the giraffe, tallest of living animals.

It is for the gold-dust and the gem, the greenfly and the gillyflower,

For the gleaming, phosphorescent glow-worm, alive with its own light.

H is for the Hawkmoth,

For the humming of its soft wings

As it hovers over flowers in the evening garden.

It is for the honeybee and the hive, for the honeybear,

And the horse champing grass in the wet fields.

I is for Icebergs,

For those massive, glittering bulks of ice

That creak and groan in the Arctic silence.

It is for the ice-floes on which the cautious seal rests,

Where the polar bear wanders, sniffing out its prey.

It is for the pack-ice that fits like a white skull-cap on the head

Of the blue and green Ark adrift in the dark.

J is for Joy and for the scent of jasmine.

It is for the jay-bird chattering in ecstasy,

For the juniper with its dark, purple berries,

For the taste of jelly-beans,

For the best joke in the world.

K is for the Kingfisher flitting across rivers,

A blue sapphire made of feathers,

Its plumage so like the colours

Of the blue and green Ark adrift in the dark.

L is for Language.

For the language of the human tongue,

For the language of the lion's roar,

For the language of the bee's dance,

For the language made by the cricket's wings,

For the language of the beating heart

Heard by a child in the mother's womb.

It is for the languages of all things that communicate

On the blue and green Ark adrift in the dark.

M is for the Mammoth, buried for centuries
Beneath a wilderness of snow and ice.
It is for the mayfly that lives a single day,
For the marigold at summer's end –
A golden button ripped from summer's coat,
Glowing in the tired garden.

N is for the Narwhal.

Thrown up onto ancient shores, the skeleton of its twisted tusk

Gave birth to the legend of the unicorn.

It is for the nuzzle of the fox,

For the nose that sniffs out danger,

For the night and its shadows creeping

Across the blue and green Ark adrift in the dark.

O is for Ocean,

For the single ocean that covers the earth.

Hardly able to comprehend its immensity,

We split it into sections and give it different names,

Its depths less known to us than the moon.

P is for the Planets –

For the planet Mars, with its red desert,

               its canyons and melting permafrost,

For the planet Venus, with its vast clouds of sulphuric acid,

For the planet Mercury, formed by the Sun's debris,

For Pluto, a tiny ball of frozen gas on the edge of everything,

For giant Jupiter, with its storms that rage a thousand years,

For Saturn, so light in density it might float in water,

For remote Uranus, for Neptune –

Earth is so unique among them.

How much more precious then the tiniest poppy-seed,

How awesome and God-like

The tiniest moth clinging to a blade of grass

On the blue and green Ark adrift in the dark.

Q is for the Quagga,

Half horse, half zebra,

A beautiful pony-sized creature

Hunted to extinction a few life-times ago.

And it is for the quelili,

The majestic brown hawk that followed it into oblivion,

Its fate the same. Now only its ghost hovers over

The blue and green Ark adrift in the dark.

R is for Rainforests.

Within them, from their dark green floors

To the tops of their cathedral-sized trees

Live half of all animal and plant species that exist

On the blue and green Ark adrift in the dark.

S is for the Stars that shiver and burn beyond the rim of the earth,

For the snowdrops drenched by spring rain,

For the nightingale's song, for the hissing snake,

For the moon-swollen seas, and the silence of underground caverns.

T is for Time,

For the twenty billion years that have melted and gone

Since our Solar System began.

It is for the thistledown blown by a child counting the hours.

It is for the tick of a watch.

It is for the tabby-cat and the tortoise

Asleep in the shade of the tulip-tree.

U is for all the Utopias unattained,

For the unborn, uncurling like ferns in the womb,

For the umbilical cord linking us

To the blue and green Ark adrift in the dark.

V is for the Volcanoes that straddle the earth's broken crust.

It is for the vibrations that run along a spider's web,

For the vampire-bat hovering over the sleeping man,

Lapping blood as gently as a kitten laps milk.

W is for Winter,

And for the wolf trotting beneath icicles hanging like catkins

In the lonely, snow covered forest.

It is for the whale and its brethren,

With their half-ton hearts beating like giant drums,

With their songs that echo across all the oceans

Of the blue and green Ark adrift in the dark.

X is for the X-rays that see what the eye cannot see,
That can peer deep into all things living
On the blue and green Ark adrift in the dark.

Y is for Yolk,

The yolk of an egg.

Yellow as the Sun, it nourishes all that the egg encloses

As the Sun's warmth nourishes all things

On the blue and green Ark adrift in the dark.

Z is for the Zodiac.

In that map of Heaven drawn with stars

We read our futures.

And it is for zero,

For the futures we will not have,

For the nothing we will become unless we cherish

The blue and green Ark adrift in the dark.

GLOSSARY

ILLUMINATED LETTERS BY SIÂN BAILEY, IN WATERCOLOUR AND INK.

The following glossary covers just a few of the interesting or unusual things mentioned in the poem and both the illuminated letters and the other illustrations. There are lots more things to spot if you look closely.

A ILLUSTRATED BY DAVID ARMITAGE IN WATERCOLOUR AND MIXED-MEDIA.

Ammonite – an extinct seashell, from the time of dinosaurs, now commonly found as a fossil. Its closest modern relative is the wonderfully named Pearly Nautilus.

Ark – the original Ark was built by Noah. God told him to build it of gopher wood and make it 300 cubits long, 50 cubits broad and 30 cubits high, with windows and a door on each side. It had three decks, each divided into compartments. Noah was told to take into the Ark his family, plus one pair, a male and a female, of every beast, bird and reptile, with enough food for all of them.

B ILLUSTRATED BY DAVID ARMITAGE IN WATERCOLOUR AND MIXED-MEDIA.

Breath – all land-living animals need to breathe to survive, taking in oxygen from the air and breathing out carbon dioxide. The balance of different gases in the air is changed by the effects of pollution and if seriously affected, can become life-threatening for some animals, including humans.

C ILLUSTRATED BY DAVID ARMITAGE IN WATERCOLOUR AND MIXED-MEDIA.

Creatures – there are over 40 million different kinds of living creatures on the Earth.

D ILLUSTRATED BY TIM CLAREY IN WATERCOLOUR.

Dawn – Every day that dawns, another three species of animal, bird, insect or plant becomes extinct.

Diamonds – exceptionally hard mineral, the hardest natural substance known. They are usually colourless, but are sometimes tinted by impurities, so diamonds can be yellow, orange, blue, brown or black.

Dinosaur – extinct terrestrial reptile, abundant in Mesozoic era. Dinosaurs lived on earth for millions of years, finally becoming extinct approximately 65 million years ago. The remains of new kinds of dinosaurs are still being discovered today.

Dodo – a flightless bird extinct since the middle of the 17th century. Dodos were found in Mauritius and its surrounding islands. The dodo had a hooked bill, short stout legs and greyish plumage. They became extinct because of the introduction by settlers of dogs, pigs and rats, which ate the Dodos' eggs. They were also hunted and killed for sport and eaten by pirates – but by all accounts they were not very tatsy.

Dove – The third bird to be sent by Noah from the Ark was another Dove, which returned with an olive leaf in its beak. This was how Noah knew the Flood was over.

Dragonfly – these predatory insects have large heads and eyes, long slender bodies and two pairs of irridescent wings, which they keep outspread when at rest. Dragonfly larvae are aquatic and can spend up to three years in water before emerging.

E ILLUSTRATED BY PATRICK BENSON IN INK LINE AND WATERCOLOUR.

Eagle – these birds of prey have large broad wings and are fairly rare in Europe now. The best place to see them is in the mountainous regions of Greece and Spain and in America.

Eggs – almost every life form on Earth starts as an egg – insects, fish, reptiles, birds, mammals.

Elements – in ancient and medieval times, people believed the universe was made up of just four elements: Earth, Air, Fire and Water.

Elephant – there are two main types of elephant, the larger African elephant, and the smaller, Indian elephant of South and South-east Asia. The African elephant was declared an endangered animal in 1989, and ivory trading was banned, but poachers are still a threat to this huge mammal. The number of Asian elephants has been depleted through loss of their habitat, as their homeland is cultivated by people who need it for farming food.

Emerald – this gem is a green, transparent variety of beryl. After diamonds, the emerald is considered to be the most precious gem.

Emu – these large, Australian birds cannot fly and are similar to ostriches.

F ILLUSTRATED BY DAVID PARKINS IN GOUACHE.

Falcon – a bird of prey, typically with pointed wings and a long tail. They are often trained by people and have been used since Roman times to hunt small game.

Flamingo – these large wading birds have pink or red plumage and downwards bent bills. They live in slightly briny or salty lakes normally. They are found in many places, including Africa, Asia, Europe, South America and the Caribbean.

G ILLUSTRATED BY TIM CLAREY IN WATERCOLOUR.

Gadfly – these large flies have a mouth and a single pair of wings that are used for piercing and sucking blood from their victim. They particularly annoy livestock such as horses.

Galaxies – the spiral galaxy that contains our Solar System, is approximately 100,000 light years in diameter.

Gillyflower – this is the old name for a carnation and is also used to describe plants with fragrant flowers such as stocks or wallflowers.

Giraffe – these large ruminant animals inhabit the savannahs of tropical Africa. They are the tallest mammals, with long legs and long necks that allow them to eat leaves from trees. Not yet classified as endangered, they are losing their habitat as their homelands are encroached upon by humans.

Glacier – a glacier is a huge, slow moving mass of ice that originates as an accumulation of snow in a cym or corrie and then overflows and moves downhill. Glaciers can move at very slow speeds, carving out the landscape as they go. Much of the landscape of northern England and Wales was caused by the movement of glaciers.

Glow-worm – these European beetles have luminescent organs that produce a soft greenish light.

Gorilla – the gorilla is the largest of the ape family and lives in the forests of West Africa.

H ILLUSTRATED BY CATHIE FELSTEAD IN WATERCOLOUR, INK, OIL COLOUR, WAX CRAYON AND BLEACH.

Hare – these solitary mammals are larger than rabbits, with long ears and long legs. They live in shallow nests.

Harebells – a plant with a slender stem and bell-shaped flowers. Also called bluebells, especially in Scotland.

Hawkmoth – the hawkmoth belongs to a family of moths with long, narrow wings and powerful flight. They can hover over flowers when feeding from the nectar and so are sometimes known as hummingbird hawkmoths.

Honey bee – a social, honey-producing bee that is widely domesticated as a source of honey and beeswax. In 1998, millions of honeybees in the UK died as a result of a virus and many hives were destroyed.

Honeybear – this animal is not really a bear, but a tree-dwelling fruit-eating mammal with a long, prehensile tail. They are members of the raccoon family and are found in Central and South America. The short-tailed ones are known as kinkajou or potto.

I ILLUSTRATED BY DAVID PARKINS IN GOUACHE.

Icebergs – these large masses of polar ice float in the sea, usually broken off from a polar glacier.

J ILLUSTRATED BY KARIN LITTLEWOOD IN WATERCOLOUR.

Jasmine – this shrub has fragrant flowers that are used for perfume and also for flavouring tea.

Jaybird – a bird of the crow family, with a pinkish body, blue and black wings and a black and white crest. They are noisy and quite aggressive birds.

Jellyfish – found in most oceans and seas, very few are poisonous. They can vary in size from a few centimetres in diameter, to several metres.

Juniper – this coniferous shrub or small tree is found in the northern hemisphere and has purple berry-like cones that are used as a flavouring in the making of gin, and also in cooking.

K ILLUSTRATED BY HELEN WARD IN GOUACHE.

Kingcups – another name for the Marsh Marigold.

Kingfisher – one of the most beautiful and most shy of Britain's birds. They usually live near open water and feed on fish.

L ILLUSTRATED BY JANE RAY IN INK, COLLAGE AND WATERCOLOUR.

Lacewing – pretty, delicate, pale green insects.

Ladybird – an insect traditionally red with black spots, but they actually come in many different colours.

M ILLUSTRATED BY CATHIE FELSTEAD IN WATERCOLOUR, INK, OIL COLOUR, WAX CRAYON AND BLEACH.

Mammoth – an extinct large elephant-like mammal, with a hairy coat and long curved tusks. Over the next 100 years more than half of all the species of animals that have ever lived on earth will have become extinct.

Mayfly – these insects begin life under water and the fragile winged adults live briefly in spring, often only for a day.

N ILLUSTRATED BY PATRICK BENSON IN INK LINE ON WATERCOLOUR.

Narwhal – the narwhal is an arctic toothed whale, with a black-spotted whitish skin. The male has a long, spiral tusk. They used to be hunted for their tusks.

Nightingale – a brownish European song bird, with a broad, reddish-brown tail, well known for its musical song, usually heard at night.

O ILLUSTRATED BY JANE RAY IN INK, COLLAGE AND WATERCOLOUR.

Oak – one of the most common and widespread trees in the UK, seen as traditionally British.

Ocean – more than two thirds of the planet Earth is covered by ocean. There are five oceans in the world, the Atlantic, the Pacific, the Indian, the Arctic and the Antarctic.

P ILLUSTRATED BY JASON COCKROFT IN ACRYLICS.

Planets – as yet, we do not know whether any other planets are capable of supporting life, but there are many planets in the known universe and the chances are that some of them are similar to Earth and so could support life.

Q ILLUSTRATED BY HELEN WARD IN WATERCOLOUR AND GOUACHE.

Quagga – this recently extinct member of the horse family looked a little like a zebra, with sandy brown colouring and zebra-like stripes on its head and shoulders. The Quagga Project, a scientific experiment set up in the last few years in Africa, has been attempting to re-create the Quagga through selective breeding of the Plains Zebra, which have the same DNA as the Quagga.

Quaking grass – this is a type of grass found in northern temperate regions and also in South America. It has delicate flower branches, that shake in the wind, hence its name, quaking grass.

Quoll – Quolls are the largest carniverous marsupials found on the Australian mainland. They have a red-brown coat marked with white spots, and very sharp teeth. They live on the ground and also in trees as they are very good climbers. Quoll is the aboriginal name for Tiger Cat and according to aboriginal legend the white spots on the quoll are spear marks.

R ILLUSTRATED BY CATHIE FELSTEAD IN WATERCOLOUR, INK, OIL COLOUR, WAX CRAYON AND BLEACH.

Rainbow – made of the colours of the visible spectrum, red, orange, yellow, green, blue, indigo and violet. After the Flood, God placed a rainbow in the sky, as a promise to Noah that he would never again send a Flood.

Rainforests – one of the most diverse and complex habitats in the world, supporting a huge number of different life forms, but under threat from commercial development, particularly in South America.

S ILLUSTRATED BY JASON COCKROFT IN ACRYLICS.

Seas – at the moment the most polluted sea in the world is the North Sea and the Irish Sea is the most radioactive.

Starfish – these are echinoderms, typically with a flattened body and five arms radiating out from a central disc.

Sun – most people believe all living things on the Earth need the Sun to survive, if not directly then because of the beneficial effects of light and warmth from the Sun. It is possible we have yet to discover forms of life that do not need the sun.

T ILLUSTRATED BY KARIN LITTLEWOOD IN WATERCOLOUR.

Tortoise – herbivorous reptile of most warm regions, with heavy dome-shaped shell and clawed limbs. They were once a very common pet in Britain, but many died while being imported. Trade in them is now tightly controlled.

Tree – trees are essential to our survival, converting carbon dioxide into oxygen. Without trees the world would be unable to sustain human life.

U ILLUSTRATED BY NICK MALAND IN INK LINE AND WATERCOLOUR.

Umbilical cord – the long flexible tube that feeds the unborn young with oxygen, food and water. It is vital for survival.

Unborn – yet to be born, life that is still to come in the future.

Utopias -an imaginary perfect world.

V ILLUSTRATED BY TIM CLAREY IN WATERCOLOUR.

Vampire Bat – bat found in tropical regions of Central and Southern America, having sharp incisors and canine teeth. They feed on the blood of birds and mammals.

Violets – a shy and increasingly rare wild flower. It is against the law to pick wild flowers in the UK now, but sadly, people still pick violets and even dig them up.

Volcano – opening in the earth's crust from which molten lava, rock fragments, ashes, dust and gases are ejected.

W ILLUSTRATED BY HELEN WARD IN WATERCOLOUR AND INK LINE.

Whale – a large cetacean mammal. Whales have flippers, a streamlined body and a horizontally flattened tail. They breathe through a blowhole on the top of their heads.

Wolf – predatory canine mammal which hunts in packs, formerly widespread in North America, Europe and Asia, but now less common.

X ILLUSTRATED BY JASON COCKROFT IN ACRYLICS.

X-Rays – a picture produced by exposing photographic film to X-rays. They are used in medicine to see things the eye cannot see on its own.

Xeranthemum – mediterranean plants that have flower heads that are dry and keep their shape and colour for years. Also called Everlasting Flower.

Y ILLUSTRATED BY NICK MALAND IN INK LINE ON WATERCOLOUR.

Yeast – any of various single-celled fungi which reproduce by budding. Yeast is used in bread making and the brewing of beer and whisky. It is an excellent source of B complex vitamins.

Yolk – the substance in an animal ovum that nourishes the growing embryo.

Z ILLUSTRATED BY KARIN LITTLEWOOD IN WATERCOLOUR.

Zinnia – plant of tropical and sub-tropical America, with solitary heads of brightly coloured flowers. Named after a German botanist who died in 1759.

Zodiac – an imaginary belt which extends 8° either side of the ecliptic. The zodiac contains the 12 zodiacal constellations within which the moon and planets appear to move. It is divided into 12 equal areas called the signs of the zodiac.